In, Out, and About Catfish Pond

By Charlotte Graeber
Illustrated by Jack Stockman

Common Sense Press
TM

Though meant to be enjoyed by itself, *In, Out and About Catfish Pond* is used as a reader in the *Learning Language Arts Through Literature 2nd Grade Red Book*, published by Common Sense Press. *Up, Down and Around the Rain Tree*, also by Charlotte Graeber and Jack Stockman, is used as a reader in that program as well.

Common Sense Press
8786 Highway 21
Melrose, FL 32666
www.commonsensepress.com

Printed in the United States of America

ISBN 978-1-880892-93-0

Rev 09/09
Printed 10/09

CONTENTS

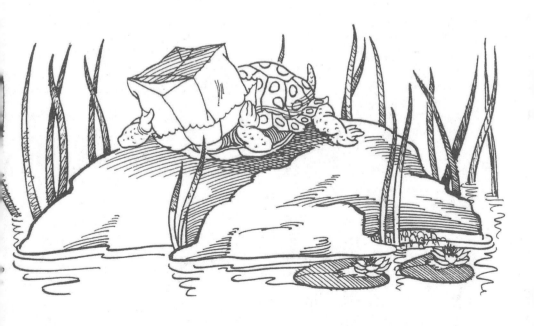

NEW SHOES, YELLOW SHOES

Clop-clop. Clop-clop. Clop-clop.
Beaver walked down the path
to Catfish Pond.
"New shoes! Yellow shoes!" he sang.
"I love my new, yellow shoes!"

Otter was fishing at the edge
of the pond.
"Good morning, Otter!" Beaver
called.
"How do you like my new shoes?"

1

Otter looked at the shoes
on Beaver's feet.
The shoes were too big.
The shoes were too bright.
The shoes were very, very yellow.
Otter did not like Beaver's
big, bright shoes.
They made Beaver's feet look like
long, yellow boats.

Clop-clop. Clop-clop. Clop-clop.
Beaver walked around and around.
"Don't you think I have the most
beautiful shoes in the world?"
Beaver asked.

"Your new shoes are very big,"
Otter said.
"Your new shoes are very bright.

Your new shoes are very yellow."

He did not wish to hurt Beaver.

"Big, bright, yellow shoes!" said

Beaver.

Clop-clop. Clop-clop. Clop-clop.

Beaver walked around and around.

"I'm glad you like my new shoes,

Otter."

Otter shook his head,

"I did not say..."

Just then Muskrat and Turtle

came by.

Beaver walked up to them.

"How do you like my new shoes?"

he asked.

Turtle put her head in her shell.

"Beaver, your shoes are too bright,"
she said. "They hurt my eyes."

"Beaver, your shoes are too big,"
Muskrat said. "Your feet look like
big boats."
Muskrat and Turtle walked away
quickly.

Beaver sat down.

"My new shoes are too bright,"
he said. "They hurt my eyes.
My new shoes are too big.
My feet look like big boats.
Why did you say you liked them,
Otter?"

"I said, 'Your shoes are very big,'"
said Otter.
"I meant your shoes seem too big
to me.
I said, 'Your shoes are very bright.'
I meant your shoes seem too bright
to me."

"But if you like the way they look,"
said Otter. "If you like
the way they fit.
Then they are just right for you,"
said Otter.

Beaver got up.

Clop-clop. Clop-clop. Clop-clop.

He walked around and around.

He sang, "New shoes. Yellow shoes.

I love my new, yellow shoes!"

"Let every one speak
the truth with his neighbor."
Ephesians 4:25

TALES ABOUT TAILS

It was washing day at Catfish Pond.

Muskrat washed his ears.

He washed his feet.

Then he began washing his tail.

"What a fine, long tail I have!"

he said.

Muskrat's black tail shone

in the light.

Close by Beaver dove into the water.

He washed his ears.

He washed his feet.

Then he began washing his tail.

"What a fine tail I have!" he said.

Beaver's wide, flat tail shone in

the light.

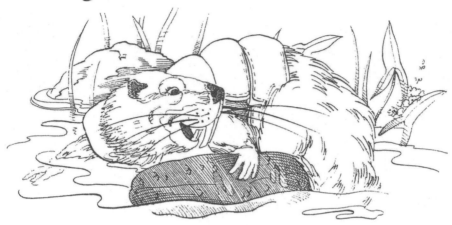

"You do have a fine tail, Beaver,"

Muskrat said. "But mine is the best."

He moved his long, thin tail

back and forth.

Swish, swish, swish.

"You do have a fine

tail, Muskrat," Beaver said.

"But *mine* is the best."
He hit his short, flat tail
on the ground.
Thud! Thud! Thud!

"I can cut a stick in two with my
tail," said Muskrat. "Can you?"

"Of course I can," said Beaver.

"And I can cut a tree down with my tail," Beaver said. "Can you?"

Otter came along the shore.
He carried his fishing pole
on his shoulder. "Good day, Muskrat!
Good day, Beaver!" he called.

"I can catch a fish with my tail!"
Muskrat shouted to Beaver and Otter.
"I can catch *ten* fish with my tail!"
Beaver shouted back.

All at once Muskrat dove
into the water. "We shall see!"
he shouted.

Beaver dove in after him.
"We shall see!" he shouted.
Otter just shook his head
and went on his way.

Splatter! Splatter! Splatter!
One long, thin Muskrat tail
hit the water.
"My tail is best!" Muskrat shouted.
Splatter! Splatter! Splatter!
One short, flat Beaver tail
hit the water. "My tail is best!" Beaver
shouted.
Splatter! Splatter! Splatter!
Water went everywhere.

At last Muskrat climbed out
of the water.

His long, thin tail dragged
behind him.
He had not caught one fish!

At last Beaver climbed out
of the water.
His short, flat tail dragged
behind him.
He had not caught one fish!

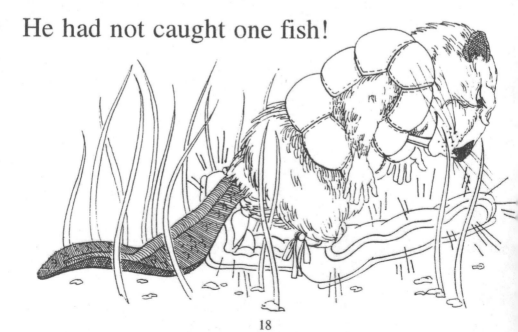

Muskrat sat down to rest.

"I cannot catch a fish

with my long, thin tail," he said.

Beaver sat down beside him.

"I cannot catch ten fish with

my short, flat tail," Beaver said.

Just then Otter walked by.
He carried a line of ten fish
over his shoulder.

"We would have fish to eat,"
said Beaver.
"If we had told the truth.
Next time we should use poles,
instead of tails."

"Do not lie to each other."
Colossians 3:9

FIVE TIMES TEN

Turtle was sitting in the sun.

Duck was swimming around and

around Turtle's rock.

"Today is my birthday," Turtle said.

"Happy birthday," Duck said.

"How old are you?"

Turtle stretched in the sun.

"I will tell you," Turtle said.

"If you do not tell anyone else."

Duck shook her wings.

"I can keep a secret," she said.

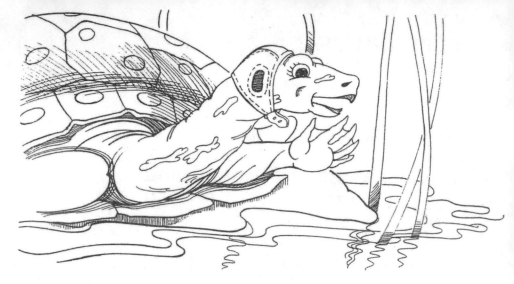

"Very well," Turtle said.

"I am five times ten summers.

I am ten times five winters."

"I will not tell," Duck said.

She shook her wings.

She swam to the middle of the pond.

Muskrat was fixing the door
on his house.

"Today is Turtle's birthday,"
Duck said.

Muskrat turned around.

"I love birthdays," he said.

"I will make Turtle a special
fish cake."

"You will need five times ten
candles," Duck said.

The words just came out!

"Oops!" Duck said.

"Do not tell Turtle I told you."

She swam to the far end of the pond.

Beaver and Otter were fishing
on the shore.
"Guess what?" Duck shouted.
"Today is Turtle's birthday."

"I love birthdays!" Otter said. "We
will pick water lilies for Turtle."
"One for each year," Beaver added.

"You will need ten times five
water lilies," Duck said.
The words just came out!
"Oops!" Duck said.
"Do not tell Turtle I told you."
Then she swam home.

That afternoon Muskrat carried a
fresh fish cake to Turtle's rock.
"Happy birthday, Turtle!" he called.
Turtle looked at the cake.
There were five times ten candles
on it.

"Thank you, Muskrat," Turtle said.
"But Duck told my secret."

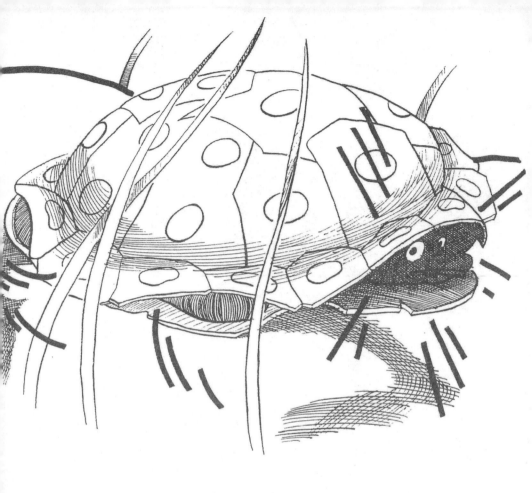

POP!

Her head was gone. Her legs were
gone. The fish cake was gone.
A green shell sat on the rock.

Next Beaver and Otter came

to Turtle's rock.

They each carried some water lilies.

"Happy birthday, Turtle!" they said.

Turtle saw ten times five lilies.

"Thank you," Turtle said.

"But Duck told my secret."

POP!

Her head was gone. Her legs were
gone. The lilies were gone.
A green shell sat on the rock.

Last of all Duck swam
to Turtle's rock.
She carried a box of chocolate-covered
water bugs on her back.
"Happy birthday, Turtle!" she called.
"Now we can have a party!"

"Duck, you told everyone my secret,"
Turtle said. Her head began to go
inside her shell.
"It just came out," Duck said.
"I did not mean to tell."

"You look young for a turtle,"
Beaver said. "Young and beautiful."

"Very young indeed," said Muskrat.

"Very young and beautiful.

You do not look ten times five to me."

"Ten times five? Five times ten?
How much is that? I can't figure
it out," said Duck.

"Never mind," Turtle said.
"I will keep things to myself from now on."

POP!

Her head was gone. Her legs were gone. A green shell sat on the rock.

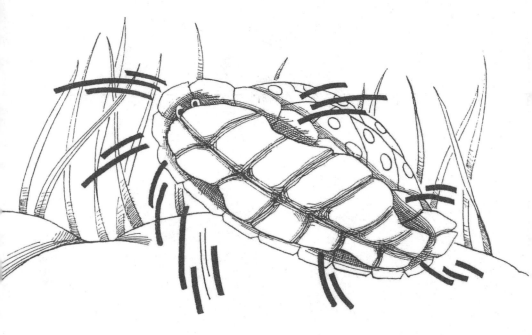

"You can tell me," Duck shouted.

"I can keep a secret."

"A gossip betrays a confidence;
so avoid a man who talks too much."
Proverbs 20:19

MUSKRAT'S FISHING HAT

"What a day for fishing!"
Muskrat said.
He put on his fishing pants.
He picked up his fishing box.
He reached in the closet for his
green fishing hat.
But the hat was not there.

"I cannot go fishing without my
hat," Muskrat said.
He looked under the bed.
He looked behind the door.
But the hat was not there.

Muskrat ran outside.

"Someone has taken my fishing
hat," he shouted.

Otter climbed out of the water.

"Who would take your fishing hat?"
he asked. "Not I."

Muskrat patted his head
with his paw.

"It must be Beaver," Muskrat said.

"He has always liked my fishing hat."

"Are you sure?" Otter asked.

"Beaver seems like an honest fellow.
I let him take care of my house
when I was away last fall," Otter
said. "I always trusted Beaver.
But maybe I was wrong."

Muskrat shook his fur.

"I know Beaver has my hat," he
said. "I am going to get it back."
He started for the far end of the pond.
Otter swam after him.

Duck was sitting in the reeds
near the shore.
"Where are you going?" she called.

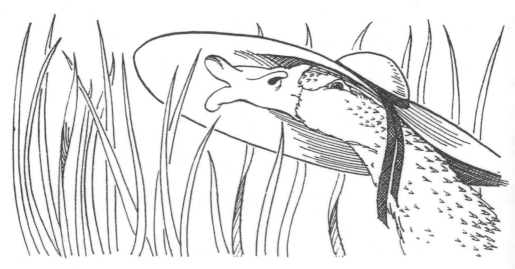

"Beaver has taken my fishing hat,"
Muskrat said. "We are going to get
it back."

Duck raised her head high
above her wings.

"Beaver seems like an honest fellow,"
she said. "I let Beaver take care of
my ducklings when I was away.
I always trusted Beaver.
But maybe I was wrong."
She swam after Muskrat and Otter.

Beaver was putting some sticks over
a hole in his roof.

"Good morning," he called.

"Where are you going?"

"Good morning, yourself, hat robber!"
Muskrat shouted.

Duck pointed a wing at Beaver.

"You have taken Muskrat's
fishing hat," she said.

Beaver climbed down from his roof.

"Why do you think I took your hat,

Muskrat?" Beaver asked.

Muskrat shook his paw

in Beaver's face.

"Well, it isn't there," Muskrat said.

"And you always liked it."

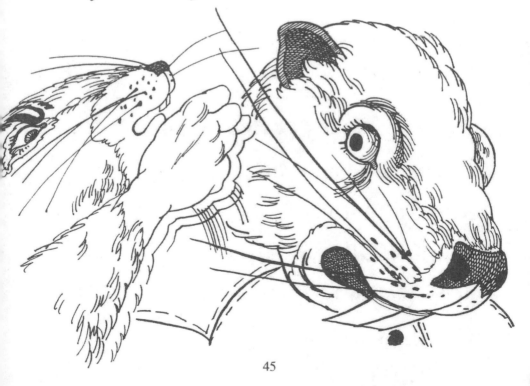

"That doesn't mean I took it,"
Beaver said.

"Look at my head.
It is large and fat.
Now look at your head.
It is small and narrow.
Your hat is too small
for my Beaver head."

Muskrat looked at Beaver's head.
It *was* large and fat.
Muskrat felt his head.
It *was* small and narrow.
"Maybe you're right.
But where is my hat then?"

"Did you look in your fishing box?"
Beaver asked.

"No, but I always keep my fishing
hat in the closet," Muskrat said.

47

He opened the box.

His green fishing hat was
right on top!

Duck clapped her wings.

"I was right to let Beaver take care of my ducklings."

Otter clapped his paws.

"I was right to let Beaver take care of my house."

Muskrat looked at his feet.

"I'm sorry, Beaver. I guess it's easy to blame someone else. Would you like to use my best fishing pole? You can go fishing today, instead of me."

"You shall not give false testimony
against your neighbor."
Exodus 20:16

THE POND MONSTER

The sun was half way behind
the willow tree.
It was time for Turtle's nap.
She popped her head into her shell
and closed her eyes.

Splash! Splash! Splash!
What is that! Turtle thought.
She popped her head out of her shell.
Otter was hitting the water
with his tail.

He was making much too much noise!

Turtle popped back into her shell.

She covered her ears with her feet.

She could hardly hear the

splash, splash, splash.

She closed her eyes again.

Turtle was very sleepy.

Clop-clop! Clop-clop! Clop-clop!

What is that?! Turtle thought.

She popped her head out

of her shell.

Beaver was walking around in his

big, yellow shoes.

He was making much too much noise!

Turtle popped back into her shell.

She put a bag over her head.

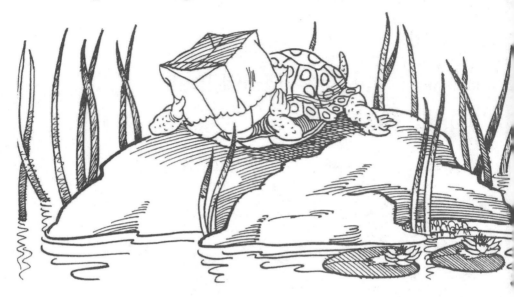

Everyone knew she took a nap
in the afternoon.
Yet every afternoon the other
animals made noise near her rock.
Turtle knew they did it on purpose.

"I know what to do!" Turtle said.

She popped her head into her shell.

She covered her ears with her feet.

Then she opened her mouth wide.

"Rrrrrrraaaaa! Rrrrrraaaaaa!"

she shouted.

Inside the shell the sound was loud.

Outside the shell the sound

was very, very loud.

"RRRRRRRRRRAAAAAAAAAA"

Otter stopped hitting the water
with his tail.
"Help! Help!" he shouted.
"There's a monster over there!"

Beaver stopped clopping around
in his big yellow shoes.
"Help! Help!" he shouted.
"There's a monster over there!
We must tell Turtle."
They swam to Turtle's rock.

RRRRRRRRRRRRRRAAAAAAAAAAAA!

The noise came from Turtle's shell.

"Who is in there?"

Beaver called.

Turtle popped her head
out of her shell.
"It is not a monster,"
said Otter. "It is Turtle."

"Why did you try to fool us?"
asked Beaver.
"We were very afraid."

"I cannot take my nap!"
Turtle shouted.
"Splashing! Clopping!
I wanted to scare you away!"

"You did not need to fool us.
We might have thrown rocks at you.
You should have told us the truth,"
said Beaver.

"I'm sorry," said Turtle.

The next day she put a sign

on her rock. It said:

And no one did.